AN
ORCA
YOUNG
READER

Danger at
The Landings

Becky Citra

ORCA BOOK PUBLISHERS

National Library of Canada Cataloguing in Publication Data
Citra, Becky

Danger at the Landings

"An Orca young reader"

ISBN 1-55143-232-3

1. Frontier and pioneer life--Canada--Juvenile fiction. I. Title.

PS8555.I87D36 2002   jC813'.54   C2002-910841-1

PZ7.C499Da 2002

Library of Congress Control Number: 2002109532

Summary: When Max is bundled off to stay with his uncle, the
miller, in an Upper Canada village, the adventure he longs for
comes when he least expects it.

Orca Book Publishers gratefully acknowledges the support of
its publishing programs provided by the following agencies:
the Department of Canadian Heritage, the Canada Council
for the Arts, and the British Columbia Arts Council.

Design by Christine Toller
Cover illustration by Don Kilby
Interior illustrations by Cindy Ghent
Printed and bound in Canada

IN CANADA
Orca Book Publishers
PO Box 5626, Station B
Victoria, BC Canada
V8R 6S4

IN THE UNITED STATES
Orca Book Publishers
PO Box 468
Custer, WA USA
98240-0468

04 03 02 • 5 4 3 2 1

*To my nephew Mark Kearns,
a great reader and writer,
for all his help on this book.*

Chapter One

"Somebody's coming!" I cried.

A birchbark canoe skimmed over the gray lake. A man in the stern paddled hard. He headed straight toward Hambone and me.

Sometimes canoes from the Indian camp came to our farm. Our friends Sarah and Peter brought us fresh salmon and berries. They visited with Papa and went home with small bags of flour and sugar and tea.

But this was not an Indian canoe. I crouched beside Hambone and put my hand on his bristly back.

Hambone was my pig. I took him everywhere. He was fat and pinky gray with small black freckles. That morning I had brought him to the lake to wash his back. Afterward I scratched his belly with a stick, which was his very favorite thing.

The canoe flew toward our farm. I could see the man clearly now. He had a black beard and he wore a bright red cap. My heart thumped. A lumberman from the logging camp!

I jumped up. I'd seen the lumbermen go past our farm lots of times, guiding their huge log rafts with their canoes. They had a camp in the forest at the end of the lake. I wanted desperately to visit them, but Papa said a lumbercamp was no place for a young boy. Sometimes Papa forgot that I was almost nine years old. He treated me like such a baby!

Kate, who lived at the farm next to ours, told Papa, "Lumbermen are wild and they drink something awful!" I kicked her leg to make her stop, but it made no difference. Papa wouldn't budge.

Sometimes, when the lumbermen poled

by on their rafts, they were so close I could see their blanket coats and colorful belts. I could hear their voices shouting out words in a strange language that Papa said was French. I always waved. They waved back, but they never stopped.

Today a lumberman was coming to our farm!

I shifted from foot to foot while the man slid the canoe expertly onto the grassy shore.

"I'm Max! The boy who waves to you!"

The man leaped out of the canoe. He thrust out his hand. "I am Pierre." His voice sounded funny, like a song.

I tried to look serious when I shook Pierre's hand. I added gravely, "And this is Hambone."

"Ah," said Pierre. He inspected Hambone carefully. "Un bon couchon."

I frowned, and Pierre said in his funny voice, "A good pig."

"Yes, he is," I said. "Very good." We both looked at Hambone. He looked back at us with his small black eyes.

A needle of worry poked at me. "He is *my* pig, but Papa named him," I said. "He named him Hambone so I won't forget. Papa says Hambone is not a pet like our dog, Star, or our cat, Pirate. Papa says we're raising Hambone so we'll have a nice fat pig to butcher."

I lowered my voice. "Papa wants to *eat* Hambone!"

Suddenly my face felt hot. Pierre would think I was a baby too! But Pierre looked horrified. He rubbed behind Hambone's ear and Hambone squeaked joyfully. That was Hambone's second favorite thing. I wondered how Pierre knew.

Then I remembered my manners. "Can I help you?"

Pierre straightened. He held out a battered tin cup. "I need some fire."

Fire! I must have looked surprised because Pierre laughed. "The rain last night." He made a whooshing noise. "Right on our campfire. Out!"

I laughed too. "That rain almost got Papa and me!" I said.

Yesterday Papa ploughed our new field. All day the plough creaked behind the tired horses. I walked behind and picked rocks. Papa had just put Billy and George in the barn and shut the door when black clouds filled the sky and the rain poured down.

I grinned at Pierre. "Come with me!"

Papa and Ellie and I lived in a log cabin on our farm. It was a fine cabin with big windows, a huge stone fireplace and three rooms. Books filled up two whole shelves. Once a man walked ten miles through the bush just to see our books.

Papa and Ellie and I had sailed to Canada on a huge ship more than two years before. It had taken Papa all that time to build our farm in the wilderness. Now we had two cleared fields, a vegetable garden, a barn for our cow, Nettie, and the horses Billy and George, and lots of stumps. I never minded the stumps, but Ellie hated them. Every spring she planted beans and pumpkins so they didn't show as much.

When I complained to Papa that I never had time for adventures, Papa laughed and said, "Coming to Canada was a great big adventure!"

"But, Papa," I protested. "That was so long ago I can hardly remember!"

We had a fine farm, and I hoped Pierre thought so too as he walked beside me. He whistled a happy tune as we followed the path from the lake to our cabin.

Star was sleeping on the porch. He stood up, hair bristling, and growled.

"Pierre is a friend," I said firmly.

Star flopped back on his tummy and watched Pierre through half open eyes. I could hear Ellie and Kate chattering through the open door. They fell silent when we entered. Ellie and Kate had been peeling and drying apples all morning. The cabin smelled sweet and delicious. Strings of pale apple rings stretched from one end of the room to the other, drying in front of the big stone fireplace. Our cat, Pirate, crouched on the floor, his eyes on the apples, his tail twitching.

"This is Pierre," I announced proudly. "He needs some fire."

Ellie and Kate stared at us. I almost giggled because they looked like fish with their mouths hanging open. Then Ellie smoothed her apron and said, "Of course."

Pierre ducked under the string of apples. He picked up two chips of wood and carefully lifted a hot coal out of the fireplace. He dropped it into his tin cup.

I wished Ellie would invite Pierre to stay for tea. I stared hard at her, but she didn't. And, for once, the cat had Kate's tongue.

"Merci," said Pierre. "Thank you." He smiled and his white teeth flashed in his brown face.

Kate gave a small squeak.

"Merci," I said boldly. I snatched a handful

of apple rings from the table and dashed after Pierre, out of the cabin and back to his canoe.

Hambone was rolling in a patch of mud by the lake. We both laughed at him, and then Pierre climbed in his canoe. He set his tin cup with the hot coal on the bottom. "Good bye, Max. Good bye, Hambone." He paddled away from the shore with strong strokes.

Ellie hollered from the cabin door, "Max! Max! You come back here right now!"

I sighed heavily. Ellie was the bossiest sister in Upper Canada.

"Max! I need you!"

She and Kate probably had a thousand nosy questions to ask me about Pierre. Or a million boring chores to make me do.

I pretended not to hear.

Pierre's canoe disappeared around the point. I sighed enviously. No one told Pierre what to do. No one made him do boring chores. He was free to have all the adventures he wanted.

I decided right then that when I grew up I would be a lumberman like Pierre.

Hambone pushed against my leg. I rubbed his ears and fed him pieces of apple. His tongue felt rough and warm on my hand.

Pierre had said that Hambone was a good pig. I struggled for the French word. A bon something.

"You're a bon pig, Hambone," I whispered with a glimmer of hope. After all, Papa hadn't talked about butchering Hambone for a long time. A very long time.

My worry melted away.

Papa must have changed his mind.

Chapter Two

"I can't eat," I said, pushing my bowl of porridge away.

"Too excited," said Papa.

He gave Ellie a strange look. Ellie and Papa had been giving each other funny looks for a whole week. They talked in whispers, and changed the subject when I came close. What were they planning? It was too early to be thinking about Christmas; besides, they looked worried, not happy.

Today, Kate's father, Mr. McDougall, was going to The Landings, and he was taking me and two sacks of wheat: one sack from our farm and one sack of his own. He was taking the wheat to the gristmill, where my Uncle Stuart would grind it into flour for our bread.

Uncle Stuart was Papa's oldest brother. He came to Canada two years before us. Papa said he mostly wandered around for a while, and then he finally settled down and built the gristmill.

It was a long way from our farm, past our lake, along a river and almost all the way down another lake that Papa called Big Lake. Before Uncle Stuart built the gristmill, there was nothing there but forest. A year later, The Landings had sprung up. Ellie had been with Papa twice, but not me. She told me there were lots of cabins and a blacksmith and a sawmill. Best of all, there was a store with peppermint candy!

I was afraid of Uncle Stuart, who was gruff and not at all like Papa, but I desperately wanted to see The Landings.

I stood glued to the window, watching the lake. Papa had said that the road was so muddy that Mr. McDougall and I would travel by canoe.

"He's coming!" I shouted. Then my heart sank. Mr. McDougall sat in the stern, and in the bow perched Mrs. McDougall, her shawl wrapped tightly around her.

"There won't be room for me," I wailed.

"Mrs. McDougall is helping me today," said Ellie. Again she and Papa traded that secret look. Then she added brightly, "And look Max, here come Jeremy and Kate running down the trail!"

Had the whole McDougall family come just to see me off? I felt very important as Papa settled me in the canoe between the sacks of grain.

"You are in charge of the wheat, Max," said Papa in his serious voice. "Our winter's bread is in these sacks."

"Yes, Papa," I answered.

"Right, then," said Mr. McDougall. He was a big, broad-shouldered man with a black beard. "We'll be back by night if the weather holds."

Papa and Mr. McDougall studied the sky. It was a clear blue November sky with a few drifting white clouds. A fresh cool breeze ruffled the water. Papa winked at me. Mr. McDougall was always gloomy about the weather, but today looked perfect.

Mr. McDougall paddled away from the shore with long hard strokes. The water streamed from the bow of the canoe in silver lines. Star ran up and down the grassy bank, barking and scaring up a flock of black ducks that paddled noisily across the water.

Papa and Ellie and the McDougalls stood on the shore and waved. I waved back until they were tiny dots. From the lake, our cabin and barn looked so small.

For a long time I watched the bags of wheat carefully, as if they might leap out of the canoe. I trailed my fingers in the water, making myself count to twenty before I yanked them out, frozen.

I tried not to squirm, but my foot had fallen asleep where it was scrunched under me. I wiggled into a new position and studied the shoreline. We were the first family to build a farm on the lake, but now I counted three more farms, brown quilt patches cut out of the dark green forest. My stomach rumbled with hunger. I thought longingly of the boiled potato and salt pork that Ellie had wrapped carefully and tucked in my lap before we left. Was it too early to eat?

"Listen Max. You can hear the river now," said Mr. McDougall. "We'll have lunch after the portage."

The portage! Papa had told me about that. The river between our lake and Big Lake was too narrow and fast for the canoe. Everything had to be carried along an old Indian trail. A sick feeling grew in my stomach. Mr. McDougall was used to big strong boys. His son Jeremy was almost sixteen, and once he walked five miles with a deer slung over his shoulders. What if Mr. McDougall expected me to carry the canoe?

But when we got close to the river, Mr. McDougall guided the canoe to the shore and shouted over the noise of the rushing water, "You'll have to stay with the wheat while I carry the canoe. It's just a mile. I won't be long." He hesitated. "You'll be all right?"

"Of course," I said, trying to hide my relief. Mr. McDougall slung the sacks of wheat on the ground beside a tree. Then, with a grunt, he hoisted the canoe upside down over his shoulders and disappeared down a narrow trail through the forest.

I sat beside the tree and eyed my lunch packet. Mr. McDougall had said we would eat after the portage. But it wouldn't hurt just to taste the potato. I unwrapped the cloth, slid out the potato and nibbled at one end. It was soft and floury and it made me feel hungrier, so I ate the other end, too. After all, I still had the salt pork. I finished off the potato in four big gulps, wrapped the pork back in the cloth, and set it on the ground.

I stared at the two bulging sacks. Being

in charge of the wheat had seemed like an important job at first. Now it was just boring.

I thought about Uncle Stuart. He had been to our farm two times. He did not look at all like Papa. Papa was tall and thin with nice eyes. Uncle Stuart was short and muscular. His eyes looked like they knew everything. He wore a shiny gold watch. Once he took it off and held it by the candle so we could see it sparkle.

After that, Uncle Stuart didn't come again. Papa said he was too busy grinding wheat at his gristmill. I got up and walked to the edge of the river. Over the roar of the rushing water, the forest behind me seemed eerily silent. I glanced over my shoulder a few times. Then I forgot about the wheat and Uncle Stuart and searched for a ship.

I found a piece of flat bark that curved up at the edges. Perfect. Setting it gently in the water, I watched the current snatch it away, scooting it past a dead snag. I ran along the shore, following my ship's wild trip through the churning water.

I was on a real ship once, when Papa and Ellie and I sailed to Canada from England. One day I would sail again, around the world. I would not come home until I had had a hundred adventures!

My bark ship hit a rock and flipped. Then it lodged itself firmly against a jam of logs and sticks that rose in the middle of the river. Disappointed, I turned to search for another ship.

I looked around. I had run farther than I thought. I couldn't see the dead snag, and I couldn't see the tree and the bags of wheat.

An uneasy feeling prickled my neck. What if Mr. McDougall had come back? What if he was standing beside the tree right now, his face dark with disapproval? What if he told Papa that I had forgotten my job?

I raced back along the river, all the

way to the tree. And then I stopped, cold horror sweeping over me.

A dark shape hunched over our bags of wheat. The rest of my lunch lay scattered on the ground, the piece of cloth ripped. I shouted, and the animal turned and glared at me with sharp black eyes. The sun glistened on its coat of smooth thick quills. A porcupine!

I knew a lot about porcupines. Once Star and a porcupine had a fight under our barn. Star crawled to the cabin, whimpering, his nose and cheeks bristling with quills. I remembered how Star's whole body shook when Papa pulled the quills out. For the first time, he growled at Papa and snapped at his hand. I had closed my eyes, and Ellie had cried and begged Papa to stop. For days after, Star wouldn't eat. He just slunk around the cabin, his face swollen and sore.

My heart thumping, I edged towards the porcupine. It had turned back to the sacks of wheat, poking and sniffing at them curiously. I imagined its claws raking through the sack, spilling our precious wheat on the ground. Papa would be furious.

I screamed, "Go away! Get out of here!"

The porcupine ignored me. It shuffled around the bags, grunting. I picked up a stout branch lying on the ground. Kate had told me that porcupines could shoot their quills, like an Indian with arrows. I swallowed hard. Papa said it wasn't true, but how could he be sure?

The porcupine clambered on top of one of the sacks. Its long curved claws glinted. I took a big breath. Then I rushed forward. I smashed the stick as hard as I could on the porcupine's back.

The porcupine grunted. It slid off the sack and spun around, its quills rising in a bristling cloud. It lowered its head and lashed its tail. I jumped back, waving the branch in front of me like a sword.

For an endless moment, the porcupine and I stared at each other. Then it gave another deep grunt, and waddled into

the forest, its tail swishing from side to side.

I waited until it had disappeared. My hands shaking, I gathered up the remains of my lunch. I sat on the ground and leaned against the tree, sucking in gulps of air to steady myself. A few minutes later, I heard a loud "Hallo" from the woods, and Mr. McDougall came striding around the bend in the trail.

I stood up. My legs wobbled like jelly. Looking after the wheat was an important job. It wasn't boring at all. But was I ever glad that Mr. McDougall was back!

Chapter Three

Mr. McDougall hoisted a sack over each of his big square shoulders and set off down the trail. Once Ellie had said, "Mr. McDougall is as strong as an ox!"

Papa had corrected her, "No, as strong as two oxen!" As I struggled to keep up with Mr. McDougall's long strides, I thought Papa should have said five oxen!

I was quiet all the way to Big Lake, hugging the secret of the porcupine to myself, imagining the look on Papa's face if he knew how close I had come to losing his grain. I could hear his disappointed voice, "Max just isn't old enough to be trusted."

A cold wind blew across Big Lake, whipping up small waves. We climbed into the canoe, and Mr. McDougall paddled down the lake, keeping close to the rocky shore. Steep forested slopes came right to the edge of the water. We skimmed past the mouths of small creeks tumbling into the lake. High above us the white foam of a waterfall shimmered in the dark trees.

"No one lives beside this lake," I said, disappointed. I decided that I liked our lake with its flat banks and grassy fields much better.

Mr. McDougall paddled into a small cove. I jumped out of the canoe onto a flat rock. Mr. McDougall hoisted the grain sacks onto the ground and pulled the canoe up onto a strip of gravel beach.

"Not much farther now, Max," he said.

I scrambled behind him along a narrow mossy trail that wound through the forest. Mr. McDougall never complained about his load, but he grunted with pleasure when at last the roof of a cabin and a brown strip of muddy wagon road appeared through the trees.

The Landings!

My eyes tried to take in everything at once as we walked through the village. Log buildings were scattered along both sides of the road. In one building, a blacksmith leaned over a glowing forge. A man with a hammer climbed over the roof of a cabin. Two Indian women wearing buckskin dresses and beaded moccasins walked by carrying baskets. A horse whinnied and everywhere was the sound of clanging and banging. A wagon sloshed by through the mud, its driver urging two tired-looking horses with his whip. The air was hazy and smelled like wood smoke.

My heart pounded with excitement. I forgot that I was tired. I wanted so badly to explore on my own. Impatiently, I followed Mr. McDougall across a narrow wooden bridge over a river. An enormous building loomed on the other side. It was bigger, much bigger, than Mr. McDougall's barn, and that was the biggest building I could ever remember seeing. I counted windows on three stories. But more surprising than that was a huge wooden wheel at the side of the building, like a gigantic wagon wheel.

"Your uncle's gristmill," said Mr. McDougall.

I knew right then that Uncle Stuart was an important man. You had to be important to own a building like that. Important, and rich!

"Stuart must be out somewhere," said Mr. McDougall. He lowered the bags of grain to the ground with a huge sigh.

"How do you know?" I said.

"The wheel's not moving. Means your uncle's not working right now. That wheel turns the stones inside the mill that grind the wheat."

"And what makes the wheel turn?"

"Water." He pointed behind the mill to a large round pond. "Your uncle's got the gates shut right now. That dams up the river and makes the millpond. When he opens them up, the water rushes through and turns the wheel. He'll show you how it works later."

"That pond's big enough to sail a boat on!" I said.

Mr. McDougall smiled. "Some of the boys in the village like to fish in there. And it's a good place to skate when it freezes."

I thought that if my uncle owned the millpond, too, he was important indeed!

I studied the huge wheel on the mill. It wasn't really like a wagon wheel at all. It had things that looked like paddles all the way around. I imagined the great wheel turning, water splashing over the paddles.

Then I sucked in my breath.

A flash of red had appeared over the top of the wheel.

And disappeared.

I glued my eyes to the wheel. A boy's head popped into sight. He had the reddest hair I had ever seen. He saw me and grinned. Then he pulled himself up

26

until he was standing on top of the wheel.

Mr. McDougall was talking to a man who had pulled up in front of the mill in a wagon. He hadn't seen the boy on the wheel.

The boy scrambled from one paddle to the next, looking down to see if I was watching. His leg slipped. I sucked in my breath. He was going to fall! He grabbed the edge of the wheel and laughed at me. His red hair flamed in the sun.

"Come up and see the view!" he hollered.

Mr. McDougall and the man turned and stared up at the wheel. A look of alarm spread across their faces.

"Or are you too scared?" the boy yelled.

"No!" My heart thumped under my winter jacket. More than anything in the world, I wanted to be on top of that wheel with the boy with the fiery hair and the big grin.

"Then come on up! You can see all the way to Toronto!"

I knew he was kidding. But I would have climbed up on that wheel with him, if I hadn't heard a voice roar behind me, "Young Red, what the devil do you think you're — "

I spun around.

Uncle Stuart was running across the wooden bridge. His boots splashed in the mud puddles. I shivered. His open coattails flapped like the wings of a crow. His face was purple with rage.

Chapter Four

"How many times have I told you to stay off the waterwheel?" my uncle demanded.

Red jumped to the ground. He squinted at Uncle Stuart. "It ain't that dangerous," he said loudly.

"Not dangerous?" sputtered Uncle Stuart. "I know millers who have lost their legs working on waterwheels."

For a second, Red seemed impressed. His bright blue eyes studied Uncle Stuart with interest. Then he sighed. "A guy can't have any fun around here."

"If you helped your ma and pa in the store more, you wouldn't be out looking for fun all the time. You're trouble, young Red. Now off you go! Get out of here!"

Before he ran down the road, Red gave me a quick wink. Red wasn't afraid of my uncle. And I had a feeling he had all kinds of adventures. I felt a pang of envy.

"And don't you be looking like that," Uncle Stuart said to me. "You don't want anything to do with that one. And don't be expecting me to give you a tour around my mill because I've got work to do."

I followed Mr. McDougall and my uncle through a door at the back of the mill into an enormous room. A pale cloud of flour dust hung in the sunlight coming through the windows. A thin-faced man with an enormous droopy moustache was stacking grain sacks against the wall. He nodded at Uncle Stuart uneasily, and then bent over a bulging sack.

In the middle of the room was a big, round, wooden contraption with a funnel on top. A wooden chute came down through the ceiling above it. I walked over and peered inside at a huge, flat, gray stone.

"That's the millstone. There's another one underneath," said Uncle Stuart. "The grain comes down the chute, through the funnel and is crushed between the stones. You stay clear when they're turning. A gristmill is no place to play."

Mr. McDougall and Uncle Stuart talked for a few minutes. Uncle Stuart wrote some things down in a big black ledger. An orange cat wound himself around my legs. I knelt beside him and stroked his rough fur. I hoped Uncle Stuart would make the stones turn before we had to leave.

"Lester, open up the gates." Uncle Stuart barked his orders.

"Can I go with him?" I asked eagerly.

Uncle Stuart shook his head. "You stay in here where you can't get into trouble."

Lester went out the front of the mill, and Uncle Stuart and Mr. McDougall disappeared through a door at the side. I stared after them resentfully. Why did everyone treat me like a baby? I could probably open the gates myself if they only let me try. After a few minutes, I wondered if they had forgotten all about me. I was just thinking that I'd like to find out what was upstairs when the whole mill shook and groaned. I jumped up, my heart thumping. The flat gray stone was turning slowly.

Boots thumped on the ceiling over-head. A stream of shiny, pale brown grain poured through the funnel. I watched fascinated as a wooden box beside the millstones slowly filled with flour.

In a few minutes Uncle Stuart was back. He had taken off his coat and rolled up his sleeves. He pinched some of the flour between his fingers, muttering softly. He cocked his head and listened.

He noticed me then and gave me a long hard look. "The stones can't rub each other. Make a spark, and the whole mill will go up in flames. Do you know how explosive flour can be?"

"No sir." I stepped back from my uncle's fierce eyes.

"Boom! That's how fast. Fire! It's a miller's biggest fear. You always have to be careful in a gristmill, you understand?"

"Yes sir."

"Now I've got work to do! Mr. McDougall's gone to the store to pick up some supplies. You can go meet up with him."

I ran out of the mill thankfully, almost tripping over the orange cat.

I picked up a handful of rocks and threw them off the bridge into the river. Then I hurried into the village. Smoke drifted from the chimneys of the log cabins and shanties. A woman stepped through a doorway and emptied a tub of water on the ground. A man chopping wood nodded at me without stopping his swing. Black and brown cows nibbled the stubble in a field behind one of the cabins.

I stopped for a few minutes beside the blacksmith and watched him press a steaming shoe against a horse's hoof. A wagon full of grain sacks pulled by two oxen rumbled past, its wheels barely turning in the mud. I crossed the road to a long wooden building with a sign saying *General Store*.

A bell tinkled when I opened the door. Mr. McDougall was hunched over a wooden counter, talking intently to a man in an apron. Behind them Red pushed a broom lazily across the floor.

Mr. McDougall nodded at me. "There you are, Max. You look around for a few minutes. I won't be long."

I didn't care how long he took. I wanted to see everything. I peered into barrels of tea and salt and molasses. One barrel was even full of axe heads, buried in sawdust, and another of glass panes for windows. Bolts of bright cloth and colored ribbons that Ellie would love crowded the shelves, along with saws and hammers, gunpowder and china dishes.

My nose tingled with the spicy smell of cinnamon and cloves and apples. The peppermint sticks filled two glass jars on the counter. I stared at them longingly. Mr. McDougall smiled. "Pick one, Max."

I took forever deciding between the stick with pink and red swirls and the one with taffy brown stripes, secretly wishing for both.

"Take the cherry one," said Red, leaning on his broom. "I've tried them all."

"Pinched them all, more like it," said his pa. He gave Red a sharp look. "You get back to your sweeping, young man."

Red sighed heavily as his pa handed me a cherry peppermint stick wrapped in a scrap of brown paper. I took it outside and sat on the porch step, sucking the end into a sharp point.

In a few minutes Red popped out beside me. He glanced over his shoulder with a satisfied grin. "Didn't see me go. Hey, you know what my pa and Mr. McDougall are talking about in there, don't you?"

"What?"

"War! Right here in Canada!"

I stopped sucking and looked at Red skeptically. I had an idea he was a pretty good liar.

"Honest. Cross my heart. My pa says there's a rebellion going on right now in Lower Canada. And any fool knows rebellion is just another name for war. Some guy called McKenzie is tryin' to overthrow our government."

I had no idea what Red was talking about. I had a fuzzy idea that the government was a bunch of men in Toronto. And I had never heard the word *rebellion*. It sounded awfully daring, trying to overthrow a government.

"Why would he want to do that?" I asked.

For a second Red looked uncertain. "I don't know why," he said in a reproachful voice. "They were whisperin' most of the time. But Pa says all patriotic men will be called to defend this country."

A shiver ran up my spine. What if Red were right? Before we came to Canada,

Papa was a soldier. Would Papa go to this war?

"I'll be going," said Red boldly. "They'll need every loyal man they can get!"

I stared at his bright eyes. "You aren't old enough to be a soldier!"

"Maybe not," admitted Red. "But I bet they'll need waterboys!"

The store door opened and a woman's voice hollered, "Red, you get back in here right now."

Red made a face. He stood up and disappeared inside.

I wrapped my peppermint stick back in the brown paper and stuck it in my coat pocket.

Red called it a war. He said he was going. And in the little time I'd known Red, I figured he would do it.

My stomach churned. It sounded like the adventure I longed for. If only I could go too!

Chapter Five

Rebellion!

What would happen to Ellie and me?

On the long paddle home across Big Lake, I thought about Papa. A long time ago on a winter hunting trip Papa fell off his horse and didn't come home. Ellie and I stayed alone for two whole nights until the Indians helped us. I remembered with a shiver how cold and empty the shanty felt. How I had longed to hear Papa's laugh and smell his pipe as I huddled in my bed.

Red said a rebellion was just like a war. Papa could be gone for months and months. If only I could be a waterboy like Red. I wasn't exactly sure what a waterboy did, but I knew I could do it.

I would march beside Papa, and I wouldn't be afraid at all.

A thought flashed through my head. Could this be Papa's and Ellie's secret? Could this be the reason they whispered and looked at me nervously? I trudged behind Mr. McDougall along the Indian trail at the portage, the canoe resting easily on his broad shoulders. Mr. McDougall seemed lost in his thoughts too. Maybe he was worried about leaving Mrs. McDougall and Kate and Jeremy.

Suddenly loud shouts broke the silence. We rounded a bend above the fast flowing river. In the middle of the current, a huge pile of logs was jammed up against a rock bar. Two lumbermen stood on the logs holding long poles. I recognized my friend Pierre and watched in horror as the log he was standing on rolled.

Pierre leaped to another log and shouted towards the shore. Two more lumbermen stood on the rocks, hollering and waving their arms.

"What are they doing?" I cried.

"Trying to get the logs free." Mr. McDougall set the canoe down on the ground. "Stay back, Max! I'll see what I can do to help."

I was always being told to stay back. Edging down the bank closer to the river, I watched the men, my heart thudding. The churning water pounded the logs against the rocks. I was sure they would never come loose. I wondered if Pierre felt the same way about his logs as Papa did about his wheat.

The logs heaved up in the middle. Suddenly, with a tremendous tearing and grinding noise, they broke free of the rocks. The lumbermen on the shore yelled.

"Pierre!" I shouted in terror.

Pierre and the other lumberman leaped from log to log. Any second they would be sucked into the foaming river. But before I could catch my breath, they had scrambled onto the bank. Water dripped from their thick beards.

I wanted so much to talk to Pierre. I

wanted to ask him if he had been scared. But he had time for only a friendly wave, and then he and the other lumbermen scrambled along the shore of the river after their logs. I watched them go.

"I'm going to be a lumberman one day," I told Mr. McDougall.

"Hmm," said Mr. McDougall.

He thinks I can't do it, I thought. Nobody thinks I can do anything exciting or brave!

When our log cabin finally came into view, my legs ached from sitting still in the cold. Smoke drifted from our chimney. I longed for Ellie's hot soup and my warm bed.

Papa met me at the cabin door. I was bursting with stories of my day, but Papa didn't listen. He stepped outside with me.

"Max," he said simply, "we butchered Hambone today."

My stomach lurched. All thoughts of porcupines and rebellion and lumbermen vanished. I stared at Papa in disbelief.

"I'm sorry," he said softly.

"No, Papa," I said desperately. "No! You changed your mind! Please, not Hambone!"

Papa tried to hug me. I shoved him hard and ran.

"Max, wait!" he shouted.

My head roared. I ran to the drying shed where Papa stored the meat. I pushed open the door. Fresh sides of meat hung from the rafters. Everything swirled around me. The smell of burnt hair and fat made my stomach heave.

I screamed.

Papa picked me up and carried me to our cabin. I kicked his legs hard and squirmed to get loose, but he held me tight.

"I hate you, I hate you, I hate you!" I cried.

Ellie looked scared. I pretended she was invisible. She was a traitor. She knew what Papa was going to do and she didn't tell me. Rudely, I shoved my bowl of soup, sloshing it on the table, but Papa didn't say anything.

I left the table, crawled into my bed and buried my face under my quilt. Salty tears stung my cheeks.

Someone sat on the edge of my bed. Then Ellie said quickly, "Hambone didn't suffer, Max. Papa did it so fast. Hambone never knew."

I stuffed my fingers in my ears.

"I cried too," said Ellie. "It's not just you who liked Hambone."

"*Loved* Hambone," I corrected Ellie in a muffled voice. "I loved Hambone."

"I know," said Ellie. She was quiet for a minute. "I'll lend you Pirate for a while."

I tried to say, "I don't want Pirate," but I was too tired.

Dimly, I felt Ellie leave.

I had two last fuzzy thoughts before I fell asleep.

They will never make me eat ham again. Ever.

Tomorrow I will run away to the lumber camp and live with Pierre.

Chapter Six

A week went by before I had a chance to run away.

Papa said that it was now December. I looked out the window at the brown stubbly field where we cut the wheat and the new freshly ploughed field, the dirt black and soft.

"Where is the snow?" I asked.

"The Indians say they can't remember a winter as mild as this," said Papa. "But snow is coming. There is ice in the bay this morning, Max, and it hasn't melted."

Ice in the bay! I didn't have much time before the lumbermen left. If only Papa didn't crowd my day with so many chores. Ellie and Papa had been especially nice to me for one whole day because of Hambone. Then it was back to work.

Every day, as I carried wood and fetched water and picked rocks in the field, I scanned the lake anxiously for canoes.

I decided that I would go to the camp today, before it was too late.

Sometimes I was sure that Ellie could read my mind. "Max, remember we're dipping candles later. You have to help me."

"I know," I said.

Inside I was thinking, When you are dipping your smelly candles, I'll be having adventures with Pierre!

Papa was in his field and Ellie was collecting eggs in the hen house when I left. My heart thumping, I ran along the trail that followed the lakeshore. I imagined Papa and Ellie hollering at me to stop, but I heard nothing except Star's distant bark.

The trail wound in and out of little bays. Most of the time you could see the lake. Sometimes the trail ducked deep into the forest. That was the part I didn't like. A long time ago, Ellie and I met a lynx on this trail.

I walked faster. If only I could have ridden George to the lumber camp. The sky was heavy with gray clouds, strangely dark for the middle of the day. My hands and my feet tingled with cold. A few snowflakes straggled down. I buttoned my coat right up to my neck and dug my hands into my pockets.

I was surprised when I stumbled into the camp. I had been expecting to hear the ringing of axes and the crash of falling trees and maybe even singing voices. When the lumbermen passed by on their rafts, they were always singing. But everything was still. The lumbermen sat around a fire in front of a long wooden shanty. They dipped bread into steaming bowls and ate hunched over.

Pierre looked as surprised as I was. He jumped up and led me to a stump beside the fire. "You have come all this way by yourself for a visit!" he said in his funny voice.

"Not a visit," I said. My eyes stung. "Papa killed Hambone," I whispered.

"Ah," said Pierre. He looked sad. "You are shivering. Come, have some soup to make you warm."

A lumberman handed me a bowl of thick yellow soup and a chunk of bread. I swallowed a tiny bit of soup and tried not to make a face. It was much too salty, not at all like Ellie's soup. I forced down another spoonful. Then I nibbled on a corner of the bread. It was hard and stale. I sighed. I would have to get used to it.

The lumbermen left the fire. They lugged bulging canvas sacks from the shanty down to the canoes at the edge of the lake. They looked tired and cold. Nobody sang.

One of the men poured a pot of water over the fire and kicked the sizzling coals with his boot.

I took one peek inside the shanty. It felt very cold. In the dim light I could

see wooden bunks along the side, like the berths we slept in on the ship from England, and a huge raised fireplace in the middle. For a second, I thought of my own cozy bed with the thick patchwork quilt.

By the time the lumbermen had everything stowed in their big canoes, the snow was falling thickly.

There were four canoes in all. I rode in Pierre's canoe. The men paddled silently down the lake, fat wet snowflakes settling on their blanket coats and caps.

When we saw our homestead, my heart thudded. I was supposed to be cleaning the barn. I wondered if Papa and Ellie had missed me yet.

Pierre called something in French to the men in the other canoes. Then he turned his canoe towards the shore. "We must say goodbye to your papa and sister," he said in a serious voice. "We will tell them you will see them in the spring."

The spring. My heart lurched. As we

paddled closer; I could see Papa, still in his field. A man on a black horse stood beside him. I strained to see who it was.

Then Papa and the man, leading his horse, walked quickly across the field. Papa held a piece of paper. I could hear him calling, "Max! Ellie!"

When Pierre landed the canoe on the beach, my stomach tightened. As I walked to our cabin, I practiced the words in my head. "Papa, I'm leaving. Papa, I'm going with Pierre. Papa —"

But Papa just stared at me, his eyes far away. Ellie came out the door. "What is it, Papa?"

Papa waved the paper. "A Proclamation from the Queen! There is a rebellion. Toronto is under siege."

Ellie's eyes widened. "What does that mean?"

Papa's face was pale. "I will have to go," he said slowly. "I must help defend our country."

Ellie gasped. Excitement grew in me.

The rebellion! Red was right!

I would go with Papa!

Then I remembered Pierre, waiting for me in the canoe. I ran back to the shore of the lake.

Pierre listened solemnly while I explained that Papa needed me. We shook hands, and he paddled out to the other canoes. He stood up and waved. I waved back. He shouted something that sounded like, "See you next year!"

"Goodbye!" I shouted.

The man on the black horse galloped down the road towards the McDougall's farm. Papa and Ellie stood in front of our cabin. Papa put his arm around Ellie's shoulders.

I ran to join them, bursting with plans.

Chapter Seven

Papa and I left for The Landings in the morning.

Papa saddled George. He tied his kit bag and his musket to the saddle strings. He swung me up first, and then climbed into the saddle in front. George blew frosty clouds into the air. He pawed the new snow anxiously. I wrapped my arms tightly around Papa's back. His rough wool coat prickled my cheeks.

Mr. McDougall had come to our cabin last night. He and Papa talked in low voices while I lay as still as a leaf in my bed, pretending to be asleep. After Mr. McDougall left, Papa walked back and forth on the cabin floor.

Thump, thump, thump went his boots. He was thinking hard.

In the morning he said, "Ellie will stay with the McDougalls. Star and Pirate can go with her. Jeremy has promised to come over every day to feed Billy and Nettie and her calf."

Ellie nodded. Her face was serious, but inside I think she was excited to be staying with Kate. I held my breath.

"Max, you will come with me to The Landings. I'll ask my brother Stuart to look after you until I get back."

I stared at Papa in horror. "But Papa!" I protested. "I would rather go to the rebellion with you!"

Ellie and Papa smiled at each other. The blood rushed to my cheeks. There they go again, I thought bitterly. They think I'm just a baby!

"Then I'll stay at the McDougall's like Ellie!" I said desperately.

"No," said Papa. "They have a house full of people right now." He gave me a stern look. "Max. No more fussing."

It wasn't fair. I wasn't fussing. And I wasn't fussing now, as we rode along the wagon road through the snowy woods, even though I could have. I was cold and tired and George's back was hard. I wasn't fussing, but Papa never even noticed.

The Landings looked different in the snow. Only a few people walked on the road. They were bundled in thick wool coats and long scarves. It was very quiet. I missed the sounds of hammers banging and horses whinnying and people shouting.

The giant wheel at the gristmill was turning. I watched the water splash over the paddles. Papa said, "The millpond is still clear of ice, but not for long. Stuart will be busy trying to get all the wheat ground before the freeze-up. You mustn't be any trouble."

Uncle Stuart *was* busy. His sleeves were rolled up and his face was dusty with flour. Bulging sacks filled the floor of the main room. Lester was tying a sack with a piece of rope. He looked at me curiously.

Uncle Stuart and Papa talked in the corner in quiet voices. I thought Uncle Stuart looked unhappy. Once, he glanced my way. I knew they were talking about me. I pretended I didn't care.

Finally, Uncle Stuart shook Papa's hand. He said, "We'll manage. But I should be going to fight too."

"The town needs its miller," said Papa. He clapped Uncle Stuart on his back. "From all accounts, we'll make short order of these rascals and I shall be back soon. Thank you again for taking Max."

I hoped Papa would talk more about the rebellion, but he didn't even take off his coat. He squeezed me around the shoulders and then he was gone.

"Put your bag in the house," said Uncle Stuart. He gave me a piercing look. "Then you can run to the store for me and pick up a package."

Uncle Stuart's house was behind the mill. It was two stories high. I couldn't imagine why one man would need such a big house. I left my bag in a small room with a glowing wood stove and a fat armchair.

I took my time walking to the store, kicking the snow with my boots. I hoped to see the friendly blacksmith and stand beside his warm forge, but the blacksmith shop was empty. He's gone to the rebellion too, I thought miserably. Everyone has gone except Uncle Stuart and me.

When I pushed open the store door, a familiar red head popped up behind the counter.

"Hey!" said Red. "I told you there was going to be a rebellion, didn't I?"

"Yes," I said, my spirits brightening. "But you said you were going!"

Red shrugged. "Someone has to stay behind and look after the women."

"Red!" shouted a voice through a doorway at the back of the store. "You keep your mind on your work!"

Red sighed. He handed me a big bulky package wrapped in brown paper. "I bet you've come for this."

The package felt like books. Uncle Stuart must be a reader like Papa! I left the store reluctantly. Red's cheery "See you around" echoed in my ears. I felt much better as I hurried back to the gristmill. Uncle Stuart probably wouldn't fuss over me as much as Ellie and Papa. Finally, I'd be able to do what I wanted. And it was great to see Red again.

As I approached the gristmill, I heard my uncle's angry voice bellowing through the open door. I froze.

"Never should have trusted you!" my uncle shouted. "Knew that the moment I laid eyes on you."

Lester ran outside, almost knocking the parcel from my hands. His face was purple. His coat hung loosely over his shoulders.

He turned and stared defiantly at Uncle Stuart who loomed in the doorway. "You've no proof!"

"I know what I saw! My watch was on the shelf this morning. And now it's gone! That's all the proof I need!"

Uncle Stuart's shiny gold watch was probably worth a small fortune!

I shivered.

"You're fired, Lester! And I'll have the magistrate after you!"

"You've no proof!" Lester shouted again, and he raced over the bridge without a backward glance.

Uncle Stuart blew his breath out in a whoosh. He seemed to notice me for the first time. He looked almost surprised. "How old are you, boy?" he said.

"Almost nine," I stammered.

Uncle Stuart smiled slowly. "Old enough to do some real work. Good."

Was Uncle Stuart going to let me pour the grain through the chute or operate the waterwheel? I knew I could do it if I just had the chance.

"You can start with sweeping. With that worthless Lester gone, I'll need all the help I can get to keep the mill clean."

My face burned. Sweeping! What was the fun in that? Besides, it was girl's work. I stomped after Uncle Stuart into the mill. Papa was probably fighting the enemy right now. Ellie and Kate were having a great time, talking their heads off. And I had to sweep my uncle's gristmill! I wouldn't even have time to see Red. Or time for adventures.

It was so unfair.

Chapter Eight

"I'll be on my way, then," said a thin woman with a tired face. She picked up the reins and clucked to her horse.

Snow had fallen for three nights, making the roads good for travel again. I watched the woman's sleigh, loaded with a sack of flour, glide smoothly over the white road.

"Uncle Stuart, she never paid you!" I said.

"She paid me with part of her flour," said Uncle Stuart. He rubbed his hands across his face. "We're finished, Max."

Uncle Stuart had been worried about beating the weather. Each morning he broke ice from the paddles on his waterwheel. All day long, the mill creaked and rumbled while the streams of golden wheat were ground into flour.

Once, I went down the narrow rickety stairs to the gear room. I helped Uncle Stuart smear greasy bear fat on the wooden gears that turned the millstones. "The friction can cause sparks," Uncle Stuart explained. "The fat keeps the gears turning smoothly."

Uncle Stuart worried a lot about fire. He liked his mill meticulously clean. I swept the floors until my arms ached. Another job I hated was checking the grain bins for weevils and beetles and mites. The orange cat kept the mice and rats away, but one morning I surprised a fat groundhog sitting on top of the grain!

Now we were finished! The mill was full of sacks of flour waiting for their owners. I was glad the ice had come. In the four days since Papa had gone, I had worked so hard I hadn't been to the store to see Red once!

I ran off now, clutching the coin Uncle Stuart had given me for a peppermint stick.

When I went into the store, I was startled to see the thin stooped figure of Lester. He was just leaving with a sack of potatoes slung over his back. He sneered at me and pushed by roughly, bumping my shoulder. I shivered. I had figured that Lester had left town.

"He hates your uncle," said Red, leaning on his usual broom. "Says he can't get another job 'cause of the lies your uncle's spreading."

Red and I stood on the porch. We watched Lester cross the road. He ducked into the door of a low log building. "That's the inn," said Red. "He'll be there the rest of the day."

"What's an inn?" I asked.

Red snorted. "Kind of like a hotel. You really are from the backwoods, ain't you?" He glanced over his shoulder into the back of the store. Then he whispered, "Come on, let's spy on him!"

We ran over to the back of the inn and peered through a dusty window. There was Lester hunched over a table. Something moved in a dark corner of the room. Three fat pigs!

I thought about Hambone and felt a lump in my throat. "What're pigs doing in there?" I whispered.

Red shrugged. Then he turned away, losing interest. He gave me a speculative look. "I've got something good in mind, but I figure you're too chicken."

My face felt hot. "I'm not!"

"Yup, you are."

"Am not!"

"I'll show you if you promise not to tell."

"I promise!" I said eagerly.

I followed Red along the road, back towards the mill. We slid down a snowy path under the bridge and trudged along the edge of the millpond. The snow got deeper and came over the tops of my boots.

At the far end of the pond, half hidden in scrubby bushes, I spotted a gray mound in the snow. At first it looked like a stack of lumber, but I could see Red had nailed some of the pieces together with long spikes. I'd seen a barrel of spikes just like them in the store, and I was pretty sure he'd stolen them.

"It's looks like an old raft," I said. I must have sounded disappointed because Red gave me an indignant look.

"It ain't just a raft." He dragged an old gray blanket from under a stack of wood. "This is the sail. It's an ice boat!"

I didn't say anything. I studied the gray pond. For the first time, the thin coating of ice covering it in the morning had lasted all day. I put my boot on the surface and thumped hard with my heel. The ice splintered and water gushed up around my boot.

"An ice boat needs ice," I said, trying to sound knowledgeable.

Red glanced at the clear, pale blue sky. "It's going to freeze hard tonight," he said in a knowing voice. "We'll have ice all right. You come back here in the morning and you can prove you're not a chicken."

I was halfway back to the mill before I remembered that I had forgotten my peppermint stick. That night I lay in my narrow bed in the small upstairs room in Uncle Stuart's big house. I could hear the ice on the pond snapping as the temperature fell.

I had a prickly feeling that Red's ice boat meant trouble. Big trouble.

I wasn't going to miss it for anything!

Chapter Nine

Red and I finished the ice boat in the morning. Red had dragged two long sled runners down to the millpond. He was very pleased with these.

"Now she'll go for sure!"

I rubbed my frozen hands together, and waved my arms to make myself warmer. The long brown stalks of grass glistened with ice crystals. The pond gleamed like a smooth stone. A fierce wind blowing off the ice stung my cheeks.

We took turns nailing the runners to the raft. The blows of the hammer boomed in the still cold air. I kept looking over my shoulder for Uncle Stuart or Red's pa but, except for a black crow hunched on a frosty branch, we were alone.

The mast was more of a problem. Red had found a tall thin pole and had nailed a stick as a crosspiece. He cut holes in three corners of the gray blanket with a knife. At each hole we tied the blanket to the mast or cross stick.

Red studied the sail and then the raft. "We need a hole in the middle of the boat to stick the mast in," he said. "But I don't see how we're going to do that."

The cold was seeping right through my boots. I stamped them on the snowy ground. "We could hammer some of those extra boards down the middle and then attach the mast between them," I suggested.

Red shot me an admiring look. We worked side by side, taking turns again. I decided not to ask Red where he had gotten the boards, or the blanket, or the sled runners, for that matter. We were down to our last spike when Red declared the job finished. We both stepped back and inspected our work. The mast tilted a little to one side. I pushed against it.

"Feels solid," I said. We grinned at each other. Red looked as excited as I felt.

We slid the boat away from shore and stepped carefully onto the ice. Red did a little jigging dance up and down. "Ice is thick," he said. "Doesn't even creak."

Red and I climbed onto the raft. We crouched down on either side of the mast and waited. The wind tugged at the edges of the blanket, but the boat didn't budge.

"We just have to get farther out," said Red. He didn't sound at all discouraged. "That's where the real wind is."

We stood on either side of the boat and pushed it over the ice, straight out from the shore. Our boots scrabbled for a grip on the glassy surface. The wind howled louder and my eyes watered. Our blanket sail billowed. We felt the boat move on its own.

"Run," gasped Red. "Don't let go!"

We gripped the sides of the boat and ran hard. I couldn't see anything because of my tears and the blowing ice crystals. Suddenly the boat was pulling us, and Red yelled, "Get on!"

With a grunt, I half fell onto the raft. I wiped the tears from my eyes. My chest ached from sucking in the cold air.

The boat zipped across the ice like a bird. The runners whirred smoothly. I figured our sail was going to blow away any minute, it was straining so hard. One of the holes started to tear. But we were flying, really flying, and that was all that mattered.

"We did it!" I yelled.

We lay on our stomachs and watched the ice skim by almost at our faces. I took a quick glance at the snowy shore. There was no one to see our great adventure, no one.

By then, we were almost in front of the gristmill. I glanced up at the windows on Uncle Stuart's house. A dark form filled one window. The back of my neck prickled.

Then Red screamed, "Look!"

A strip of dark water! We were heading straight towards it!

An icy wave of fear washed over me. "Stop the boat!"

"Can't," said Red. "Don't know how!"

The black water swept closer and closer. I squeezed my eyes shut against the screaming wind.

"Jump!" said Red.

We rolled off the raft at the same time. I hit the ice hard, my breath escaping with a whoosh. Ice crystals scraped my cheek. I heard Red grunt. Carefully, I hoisted myself onto my elbows. Stricken, I watched our ice boat fly into the open water. It landed with a splash and leaned heavily to one side.

I sucked in huge gulps of air. My heart hammered against my chest. My shoulder ached where I had slammed into the ice. Dimly, I heard voices shouting. Uncle Stuart and some other men stood at the edge of the pond. Uncle Stuart held a long ladder.

I pulled myself up on my knees.

"Stay down!" Uncle Stuart yelled. "The ice!"

I looked around slowly. The ice was different here, not smooth and clear like where we had started. It was blue-gray. Water gurgled under the surface. My stomach lurched with fear. Beside me, Red sucked in his breath.

"Lie flat!" Uncle Stuart hollered. "Take it slow!"

We inched on our bellies over the bad ice. It took forever. I thought I could hear the ice cracking underneath us. I could feel the cold black water sucking us in.

Uncle Stuart shouted, "Take it easy! Take it easy!' When we got close, he slid the ladder towards us. We grabbed the end, and Uncle Stuart and another man pulled us in.

Uncle Stuart was white with fury. "How could you be so stupid! The ice is always thinner by the mill ... any idiot would know that ... I promised ... Your papa would never ..."

He choked on his words. I stared at a clump of snow, my stomach churning.

"Into the house!" he finally bellowed. "And Red, go home! And don't think your pa won't hear about this!"

My legs wobbled like jelly, but Red looked surprisingly calm. Before he ran off, he confided in a quick whisper, "I'll get a licking for sure! But it was worth it!"

Uncle Stuart banished me to my room. I sat on the edge of the bed and stared out the window at the millpond. The ice turned pale pink and gold and then, finally, black as the sun set behind the forested hill.

It had been the best feeling in the world — zooming across the ice on our boat, the wind blowing on my face, Red laughing beside me. For one wonderful minute, it had been the greatest adventure ever. Like everything else, it had gone wrong. Why did Uncle Stuart have to get so angry? It wasn't our fault the stupid ice was thin.

I kicked the floor. Why did there have

to be a stupid rebellion? Why did I have to stay with Uncle Stuart? It was so unfair.

Thump, thump, thump. Uncle Stuart's boots pounded up the stairs. My stomach twisted into a knot. He opened the door. He set a plate of bread and cheese on a small table. His eyes were cold.

I pretended I was Red. Red wasn't afraid of anything. "How long do I have to stay in here?"

Uncle Stuart's eyes never flickered. "Until your papa comes back!" he thundered. He slammed the door.

Until Papa comes back!

His boots thumped down the stairs. The front door crashed shut. I ran to the window. A full moon washed the snow in white. Uncle Stuart's shadowy figure strode over the bridge and along the road until he disappeared around the bend.

Until Papa comes back!

I took a deep breath. I had to plan my escape.

Chapter Ten

My head whirled with plans.

I would leave at once to join Papa in the rebellion. I had a vague idea it would take me many days to find Papa. I would have to build shelters under trees at night. Once Papa had stayed out for two nights in the snow. He had made a bed out of spruce branches. I would do that, too. I imagined the looks of surprise and admiration on everyone's faces.

"Max stayed out all night," they would say. "That Max, he can do anything!"

These thoughts tumbled around in my head as I packed my bag. I wrapped the cheese and bread in my extra shirt, pulled the thin quilt off the bed, scrunched it into a ball and stuffed it in the top of my bag.

I took one last look out the window and blew out my breath in relief. No Uncle Stuart striding over the bridge. Nobody at all. In the moonlight, the gristmill loomed huge and shadowy.

I stiffened.

Something had moved in the shadows by the back door of the mill.

I pressed my face against the cold glass. Nothing. A dog nosing around, looking for scraps, I told myself. Or the orange cat out mousing.

Then a dark figure slid away from the door. A light flickered. Now I could see that it was a man, wearing a bulky coat and carrying a lantern. I frowned. What a strange time to come to the gristmill.

The man moved slowly around the side of the building, stopping to peer in the windows. He turned and stared up at Uncle Stuart's house. The moonlight shone on his thin face and droopy moustache.

My breath caught in my throat.

Lester!

Lester, with his muttered threats and mean eyes. I stepped back from the window, held my breath and waited, my heart pounding. Then I took a deep breath and slid back to the window.

Lester was standing by the door again. He looked up at the house one more time, then disappeared inside the mill.

I swallowed uneasily.

Lester must have forgotten something. A scarf or his gloves or ...

But why would he come now, in the cold night when the gristmill was dark and closed up? I shivered. I looked back down the road, almost wishing that I would see Uncle Stuart striding back, his coat tails swinging.

"Lester is here to see you," I would shout, and then it would be over, this prickly feeling that something was terribly wrong.

What should I do?

The door opened and Lester slipped outside. The lantern swung at his side. I strained to see if he was carrying anything else. He was hunched over, hurrying, and I couldn't tell.

When he got to the bridge, he stopped and stared back at the gristmill. He looked like he was frozen for a second, and then he broke into a run. Had something scared him? I looked back at the gristmill.

A light flickered in one of the dark windows.

For a wild second, I thought Uncle Stuart was inside, counting his sacks of flour.

But Uncle Stuart had gone the other way. I had watched him hurry down the road into the village, intent on his business.

I frowned. Lester must have lit a candle and forgotten to blow it out. How many times had Uncle Stuart warned me about the danger of fire? He would be furious.

The flickering light grew. Orange light danced behind the black window. I felt myself go very still. It wasn't a candle. It was a fire. The gristmill was on fire!

I leaped down the stairs, jumping two at a time, and ran outside. "Fire!" I screamed. "Fire!"

The night was still and quiet. My breath made a frosty cloud. A tree snapped in the cold.

My stomach heaved. "Please, somebody come! Fire! Fire at the gristmill!"

Chapter Eleven

I pushed open the heavy wooden door. The orange cat shot between my legs, his fur bristled, screeching in fear.

Fire!

In the middle of the floor, yellow and orange flames crackled and snapped, shooting sparks into the air. A haze of gray smoke hung near the high ceiling.

I covered my face with my hands. The flames danced on the huge millstones and the sacks of grain stacked neatly around the walls. Strange shadows flickered in the dark corners.

I edged closer to the fire, fighting back my terror. Smoke stung my eyes and tears slid down my cheeks. I could make out a pile of thin sticks, cracking fiercely in the flames. A heap of grain sacks, strewn beside the burning sticks, smoldered around the edges.

The back of my neck prickled. Lester had set the fire on purpose! He was trying to burn down Uncle Stuart's gristmill!

Uncle Stuart's warning rang in my head, "One spark and the whole mill can go up in flames. Do you know how explosive flour can be?"

Explosive ... explosive ... explosive! My heart pounded. I tried to fight back my panic.

Think!

Uncle Stuart always kept a bucket of water outside the back door for emergencies. Relief flooded through me as I ran for it. I covered my mouth with my hand and breathed through my fingers.

I flung open the door and sucked in a gulp of fresh air. Then I reached for the bucket. It was solid with ice. I kicked it hard against the side.

Run! I thought. Run away before the mill explodes! Run to the village and get help!

Papa's grain was inside the mill. Papa's grain and the McDougall's and all our neighbors' and friends'. "A year's hard work," Papa said when the last of the wheat was threshed. "Our bread for the winter, Max."

I filled my lungs with air and edged back inside the mill. I could try to save at least some of the grain. I tugged desperately at one of the bulging sacks leaning against the wall. Grunting, I slid it along the floor. Something glinted on the wooden floorboards. Uncle Stuart's gold watch! I stared at it in shock. Somehow it had fallen down behind the grain sacks. Lester hadn't stolen it at all! No wonder he hated Uncle Stuart so much. Trembling, I slipped the watch into my pocket.

With one last tug at the heavy sack, I gave up in despair. The heap of empty sacks and sticks was burning hard now.

Orange flames shot towards the ceiling. A sudden picture jumped into my mind. Last winter, a spark flew out of our fireplace right onto the dry bristles of Ellie's broom. The broom burst into flames. Papa took a heavy wool blanket and threw it over the broom. "Smother a fire, Max," he had explained as I watched in fear. "That's the best way."

"Smother a fire," I repeated to myself as I searched for something, anything to throw over the flames.

Nothing. *Nothing*.

My coat. I pulled off my mittens. My fingers fumbled over the stiff buttons. I finally dragged the coat over my shaking arms. I rubbed my streaming eyes and then, stepping as close to the roaring flames as I dared, I flung the coat over the burning sacks.

Run!

I stumbled through the door. For a second I stood frozen, breathing hard. Then I raced over the bridge toward the village.

I banged on shanty doors, screaming "Fire! Fire at the gristmill!"

I kept running. My breath was ragged and the biting cold stabbed my chest through my shirt. I ran until I reached the inn.

I pushed open the door. The room was hazy with smoke. A woman and three children huddled by the open fireplace, bent over steaming bowls. Some men sat at a long wooden table. I could smell the pigs and whisky and roasting meat.

Uncle Stuart jumped up from the table. "Max! What are you doing here? You look half-frozen. Where is your coat?"

"Fire!" I gasped. "At the gristmill."

Horror flooded Uncle Stuart's face. Suddenly the room was full of shouting voices and movement. Someone pulled a thick coat over my stiff arms and then forgot about me. I ran outside after the men. We raced down the road, joined by the few men that were left in the village and women and boys pouring out of the shanties and cabins. Some pulled

on coats and hats and gloves as they ran.
Axes and buckets swung against their legs.

I ran as hard as I could and caught up to Uncle Stuart. He cried out as the mill came into sight, the windows glowing orange in the black night. My coat had not stopped the fire.

Quickly, the people organized themselves. Some went inside the burning mill and others formed a line outside. One man smashed his axe into the ice on the millpond. Grim-faced men and women filled buckets with water and passed them along the line into the mill. I squeezed into a spot and helped swing the buckets along. The icy water sloshed on my knees and soaked my mittens.

Just when I thought my arms would fall off, I heard a great cry from inside the mill. "It's out! The fire's out!"

We all burst into shouts. The man beside me thumped me on my back.

Uncle Stuart stumbled outside. His face was blackened by smoke. "We saved it," he announced in a hoarse voice. "Not one sack of flour lost."

The men cheered again. Then Uncle Stuart saw me. He stared hard with his dark eyes. "Max, what happened?" Exhaustion washed over me. I stumbled over my words. "Lester ... I saw him ... the bucket was frozen. I used my coat. Papa said to smother a fire ..."

My words dwindled away. I felt overcome with cold and tiredness. I wondered dully if I would get in trouble for leaving my room.

Then I realized that all the men had fallen silent. They were looking at Uncle Stuart.

"I didn't stop the fire, Uncle Stuart," I said in a tired voice. "I'm sorry."

"But you slowed it down," said Uncle Stuart. "Until we could get there. You saved the mill, Max."

"You have a brave nephew, Stuart!" someone called out. Uncle Stuart stepped forward. He took my hand and shook it solemnly. "Yes, I do," he said in a hoarse voice, "I do indeed."

Papa and the other men rode back to The Landings the next day.

"The rebellion is over?" I said. I was half excited to see Papa and half disappointed that it hadn't been a real war after all.

"It was mostly over when we got there," Papa admitted. "That's the last we'll see of that rascal McKenzie."

My face fell. "So you didn't get to be a hero?"

"No," said Papa. "There was nothing much to do."

I studied Papa's face to see if he minded. He smiled back at me. "I think one hero in the family is enough," he said. I felt my cheeks turn red with pleasure.

Papa was anxious to get back to our farm. He turned down Uncle Stuart's offer for us to spend the night. Red came to see us off.

"I can't believe I missed it," he moaned for the hundredth time. "The best thing that's happened and I slept through it. I wonder if there'll ever be another fire?"

"I hope not!" said Uncle Stuart, but he smiled at Red.

"What will happen to Lester?" I asked.

"He's long gone," said Uncle Stuart. A shadow crossed his face. "I judged him wrongly and I'm sorry for that." He went on, his watch glinting on his wrist, "Someone saw him riding out of town in the middle of the night. I won't be sending anyone after him."

Papa squinted out at the frozen pond. "That's an odd thing out there. What is it, Stuart?"

We all stared at the ice boat, tilted sideways and frozen fast in the ice. Uncle Stuart frowned, but I didn't think that he was really mad. "Max can tell you all about it on the way home."

Red nudged me. "Our boat will be there until spring," he said in a satisfied voice.

"It would make a perfect pirate ship," I said.

Red's eyes sparkled. "I'll make a skull and cross bones!"

"You have to wait for me," I warned him quickly.

Red hesitated.

"It was my idea!" I said firmly.

Red grinned. "Agreed."

He spat two times on the snow. We shook hands.

Then I climbed onto George's back behind Papa and waved to Uncle Stuart.

"Come back soon!" Uncle Stuart called. "I can use another man around the place!"

"Only if I can spare him!" Papa called back.

George set off at a fast trot, kicking up snow with his hooves. All the way home, I told Papa all about my great adventures.